333 Middle Diablo Part 1

The Beginnings of The Story About a Crimson Warrior

Sebastián García

333 MIDDLE DIABLO
Part 1
The Beginnings of The Story About a Crimson Warrior

Edited by: Corporación Ígneo, S.A.C.
for his publishing label Ediquid
José Olaya 169, Ofic. 504, Miraflores. Lima, Perú
First edition, February 2025

ISBN: 978-956-6404-12-5
Print run: 50 copies

It finished printing in February 2025 at:
ALEPH IMPRESIONES SRL
Jr. Risso Nro. 580 Lince, Lima

www.grupoigneo.com
Email: contacto@grupoigneo.com | Contact number: +51 955 071 270
Facebook: Grupo Ígneo | X: @editorialigneo | Instagram: @grupoigneo

Collection: Nuevas Voces

Content

To my father who,
despite not always understanding me,
has always supported me.

Chapter I
The Flame Ignites

On a small floating island in the middle of nowhere, there is only a dry tree, two crows, and a man in a white kimono playing a ukulele.

I know what you're thinking: "Why is he playing a ukulele and not a lyre?" Just kidding—I know you're not wondering that, but I'll take the opportunity to say that lyres are out of fashion. Let me introduce myself: I'm Vicen Beatun, the celestial narrator. I see everything happening right now in both worlds. Like that man in London who dropped a sardine and cheddar cheese pizza on the floor and still ate it. Gross!... Sorry, I got sidetracked. I'm going to tell you, as it happens, a great story that has everything—from demon toads to a killer rabbit with an eye patch. The questions you have now will be answered little by little. Let's begin.

The bell announcing summer vacation has just rung at a high school in Montevideo, Uruguay. Exiting the building is a red-haired girl dressed in jeans and a synthetic leather jacket. She is our protagonist, a fifteen-year-old teenager named Lucí Fernández. A little further away is a slim blond boy talking on the phone. He is Lancelot Torres, her lifelong best friend.

"Lanza!" calls Lucí, using the nickname she gave him (she gives original nicknames to almost everyone).

"Huh?" he says, turning in her direction. "Oh! Oh... hi, Lucí..."

It turns out the boy is a scaredy-cat and shy, even more so when he's with Lucí, whom he's ultimately in love with. She knows it but is still thinking about how to respond.

"I'll call you in five minutes, Mom," says Lance, ending the call.

"Is something wrong, Lanza?" asks Lucí, noticing the boy is nervous.

"N... nothing, it's just that my mother said that..." He pauses a bit. "My mother said I should be ready soon because tonight we're going to visit my grandfather, who lives far away."

"The 'Karate Grandpa'? The one you say has a dojo and teaches you karate, right?"

"Y... yes, that's him."

"You always talk about him, and I've never met him."

"I... it's... it's just... he has trouble traveling. You know how my motion sickness is, but in his case, it's worse," he tells his friend.

"How is it possible that your whole family has motion sickness!?"

"Let's just say it's hereditary from my mother's side," laughs Lance.

"So, your kids will have it too, right?" adds Lucí mischievously.

"Yes," Lance responds, but suddenly, his face turns redder than a tomato. "Uh... see you later!" he says, running away.

"Hee, hee, hee," laughs Lucí at Lancelot's reaction, which she saw coming from a mile away.

As she heads home, Lucí feels a bit jealous of her friend. He always visited his family in another country whenever he could, while she barely had any relatives—just her mother and her aunt (her mother's sister). She was an only child. Her father was an orphan and died when Lucí was just three years old, and her mother's parents had died a few years before as well.

Although she felt she had moved past it, she sometimes felt sad when she thought about it.

When she arrives home, her mother, a slim woman with black hair and just a few centimeters taller than her daughter, greets her with a hug. She had a habit of hugging so tightly that a couple of bones would crack.

"Oops, sorry, Lucí! I overdid it again with the hug," her mother apologizes.

"It's okay, Mom, I like it!" clarifies Lucí. "How about lunch?"

"Lunch is ready."

Her mother points to the table, which is laden with seafood dishes, including her favorite food—octopus—for the main course. Without much delay, Lucí starts devouring her lunch like a beast.

"Great, a feast to celebrate the start of the holidays. Thanks, Mom!"

But she notices while eating that her mother seems uneasy.

"Is something wrong, Mom?" Lucí asks, her mouth full. "You look worried."

"No, nothing, dear," her mother replies, quickly changing her expression. "Actually, I have something for you."

"Really? What?" the teenager inquires, still with her mouth full.

Her mother places a wooden box on the table, opens it, and takes out a bracelet with a fire-red stone.

"And that?" Lucí asks, now with her mouth empty.

"It belonged to your father. For him, it was like a lucky charm. And I would like it to be yours..."

Lucí is surprised by this.

"Wow, I didn't expect this, but sure, Mom, I'll always wear it," she says, putting it on her right wrist.

The following day, she suddenly stops on her way to the supermarket. She feels something strange in the alley beside her. She doesn't know what it is but heads there, intrigued. When she gets halfway down the street, a column of fire bursts from the ground behind her, leaving her stunned.

The flame lasts for about two seconds and then disappears. Lucí is confused and scared.

"Holy carrion! What's happening?"

And then she hears a voice out of nowhere:

"Miss Lucí! What a relief to have found you!" says the unknown voice. "One more second, and you would have been lost!"

Lucí doesn't understand anything that's happening.

"Who are you, and where are you!?"

"Miss Lucí, touch the stone on your bracelet," explains the voice.

"How do you know about my father's bracelet?" asks Lucí, confused. "And why do you want me to touch it?"

"Just touch it!" the voice insists.

"Okay, okay, I'll touch it," Lucí agrees.

She follows the order and thinks, "As if touching it would make me see you."

However, after touching the stone, she sees a floating fireball with two eyes.

"Holy carrion! What the devil are you!?" asks Lucí, surprised and shocked.

"I am Fatuo, and I am not a devil, so..." says the fireball, but he can't finish because Lucí interrupts.

"'Devils' is just a figure of speech!" she shouts irritably. "What was that fire!?"

"I launched it to protect you from..." but he can't finish because something appears at the end of the alley, "...from a demon like the one behind you now!"

"Huh!?"

Lucí turns around and finds something unbelievable: a five-meter-tall anthropomorphic pig about to hit her with a giant club.

Fatuo gets serious and says, "I'll han..." but again doesn't finish because a scream comes from the beginning of the alley.

"Nobody messes with milady!"

As the voice says this, a spear is thrown into the pig's forehead, making it step back.

"Wait... What!?"

Lucí recognizes the voice but has no time to think further. The pig stands up only for a moment because the attacker approaches where the spear is stuck and pushes it deeper with a foot, piercing through, while saying, "And if you do, you'll feel my fury!"

Lucí is petrified. It turns out to be Lancelot, dressed in light armor like a medieval knight, with an emblem of what appears to be a blue flame on his chest. Unlike yesterday, he seems brave and confident, like someone else.

The demon pig falls on its back and starts disintegrating into crimson ash. Lance extends his arm with an open palm, and the spear returns to his hand. When he grabs it, Fatuo says:

"For the record, kid," he says arrogantly, "I could have handled this perfectly well on my own."

"Sure, the damn pig was about to hit you guys," he finishes the thought with sarcasm, "...but you were fine alone..."

Lucí approaches them.

"Excuse me..."

"Sorry, miss, but the kid..." starts Fatuo.

But suddenly, Lucí gets furious and shouts, "For Everest's sake! Can someone tell me what the carrion is going on here!?"

From the fear, Fatuo and Lancelot hug each other (actually, Lance hugs Fatuo because Fatuo has no arms, and since Fatuo is made of fire, Lance burns his arms and hands a bit).

The scare makes Lance return to his usual self.

"I... it's... it's just... that... that..." Lance stammers, but he's not the only one.

"Mi... miss... Lucí..." Fatuo stutters as well.

"Please, tell me what the carrion is happening!" Lucí demands.

But before they can respond, they feel an intense wind behind them and hear an exclamation, "Armadillo whacker!" followed by a solid thud.

Turning around, they see a kind of giant tiger with torn pants lying on the ground, unconscious. A spiked mace with a long chain is embedded in its head.

The tiger begins to disintegrate, just as the pig did.

The mace chain winds up like a fishing rod until it reaches the handle. Now looking like a regular mace, it is held by a blonde woman dressed in a gray kimono with spikes like those on the weapon.

"Darling, stay more alert in an emergency like this," says the woman.

Upon hearing her, Lance stands firmly, letting go of Fatuo.

"Yes, Mother, I'm sorry..."

Lucí immediately recognizes her. She is Lancelot's mother, Nimue, who turns to her:

"Are you okay, darling?"

But Lucí is still furious and confused.

"Mrs. Nimue, what is happening here!?"

There are a few seconds of silence. Everyone except Lucí has a depressed face. Nimue breaks the silence when she explains:

"It's time you knew the truth, Lucí."

Lucí goes from angry and bewildered to just bewildered and asks, "What do you mean, the truth?"

"Lucí, I know it's going to be difficult, but I need you to listen carefully and believe what I say," Nimue begins.

"What do you mean?"

"If you can, don't ask questions until the end."

Nimue begins her explanation:

"You see, the Earth is connected to a spiritual world called Nirma, where demons live, but also humans who can see and be in that spiritual plane. Nirma only has a spiritual side. On Earth, common humans are in the physical space, and the spiritual side almost doesn't interfere with it. Demons can only be on the spiritual plane, at least the red ones, who are the evil demons, like the ones that just attacked you. The 'good' demons can pass to the physical side and blend in with humans."

Nimue pauses her explanation.

"Any questions you think are important to ask?"

Lucí indeed has many, but she chooses the most significant one.

"Yes, why did all this happen suddenly?"

Nimue thinks, "I'll tell her straight".

"Today, there was a breakout from Tartarus, the prison of the red demons. After they killed the warden—the strongest in both worlds—almost all the demons inside escaped, and it seems they want to come for your head."

Lucí is stunned by this revelation.

"And why do they want to kill me?"

Then Nimue, Fatuo, and Lancelot start to cry.

"What's going on?" insists Lucí, still not understanding.

"It turns out that demon..." Nimue says, bursting into tears, "was your father."

Lucí is shocked by this.

"No... it can't be. He died twelve years ago... didn't he!?"

Nimue is inconsolable.

"It's a long story. We'll tell you more in a safe place."

But Lucí reacts vehemently:

"I don't care about safety! Tell me!"

Fatuo gathers the courage to speak.

"Twelve years ago, Natas captured a demon that had been looking for you for some reason since you were a baby. When he sent it to Tartarus, it was so strong that it caused a massive breakout. And since Natas was the most powerful demon, he was appointed warden to contain that escape and get answers from that being."

Then he starts crying even more.

"He never got them, and since yesterday, the demon was using more force than ever to escape. We controlled it but didn't count on it receiving external help from another demon. There wouldn't have been a breakout if it weren't for him."

"I'm very sorry, Lucí. We should have told you earlier," says Lancelot through tears.

"No," intervenes Lucí with her head down. "It's not your fault... My parents... should have told me. I had already accepted my father's death twelve years ago, but not that they had lied to me my whole life!"

Lucí, unlike the others, is not only sad but also furious.

Suddenly, a demon snake with arms appears, approaching them. Lucí sees it and angrily shouts:

"Get lost! I'm not in the mood..."

As soon as she says this, the snake's entire body catches fire, and, like the previous demons, it begins to disintegrate.

Lucí is stunned by what just happened.

"What was that?"

"It was your enchantment, Lucí," explains Nimue, surprised.

"Enchantment? What do you mean?"

"An enchantment is the innate power of most demons or a human with vision, meaning someone who can see and be in the spiritual plane," describes Nimue. "Each person's enchantment can vary; they can be inherited or depend on the user's soul when it awakens."

Then, Lucí notices that her bracelet is glowing.

"Does this bracelet have something to do with it?"

"It's an 'anchishiru,'" explains Fatuo. "It's a magical device that allows its user to activate their enchantment and move to the spiritual side if their aether is sealed, which is the energy a holder of an enchantment needs to use it and go to the spiritual plane."

"So, since my father was a demon and my mother a human, it means I'm a mix of both," concludes Lucí, "which allows me to have powers, right?"

"Yes, Lucí, that's correct," says Fatuo. "You have the 'blossoming fire' enchantment, one of the most intense fire enchantments."

"And the red demons are after me because of my power?"

"We assume so..." replies Nimue.

But just as Lancelot's mother finishes saying this, Lucí runs out of the alley.

"Where are you going, Lucí!?" Lancelot asks nervously. "The red demons are looking for you!"

Lucí responds without stopping.

"Well, now I'm looking for them!"

Chapter II
Big News

Lucí runs down the street searching for demons. After a couple of blocks, she finds, in the physical world, a car crash at an intersection. And, in the spiritual plane, five red frog-like demons, each the size of a bear.

Before the frogs notice her, Lucí runs toward them, ignites her fist in flames, and punches one in the back—*fire punch*! —sending it like a fireball into a building.

The other four demons react and start moving toward her. The first one that tries to attack her, she dodges and kicks—*bottom burn*! —sending it flying away.

The second one jumps at her, but she grabs it by a leg with both hands in mid-air. Before it can do anything, Lucí starts spinning around with the frog still in her grip—*spinning fire*! —she turns quickly and sets the frog on fire with her hands, leaving a trail of flames. When another frog approaches, Lucí stops and throws the one she's holding—*rocketto launch*! When the frogs collide, they explode in a giant blaze.

The last one tries to attack her from behind, but it's out of luck because Lucí notices and punches it downward with a red war hammer, making it literally bite the pavement.

When she thinks she's done with them, a wave of demons comes from all directions, but Lucí doesn't flinch. She creates a fiery bubble around herself, then explodes, forming a fire shockwave —*expansive crimson!*—pulverizing half of the demons it reaches.

In the physical plane, the car crash has already been cleared, and the drivers have been taken away, one of them with a fractured arm. The intersection is back to normal. Meanwhile, on the spiritual side, there's a fire about a thirty-meter radius caused by Lucí's demon massacre.

As entertaining as the fight is—so much so that Ginn and Minn, my pet crows, have started eating popcorn—I'm heading to the rooftop of a nearby building, where Lancelot and Fatuo are watching the carnage.

"Well..." says Fatuo, "this is going to take a while. I'm going to watch all *the Lord of the Monkeys* movies," and he turns around.

But Lancelot hits him, leaving a bump... Wait, how can a fire demon get a bump? ... Well, never mind. Let's continue.

"How can you joke at a time like this!?" Lance yells at him angrily, "especially after the death of Master Natas, who was your best friend..."

"That's exactly why..." Fatuo starts crying, "He wouldn't have wanted us always to be sad, but to move forward and turn our tears into smiles!"

"Look who's talking. You just started crying!" Lance says, smiling while looking down a bit depressed. "I hate to admit it, but you're right. As Master Natas would say: 'Don't look at the causes of a problem, but the way to solve it.'"

Since he doesn't have a mouth, Fatuo smiles with his eyes.

"Despite being a kid, you do know how to listen..."

"Look who's talking, floating fire..." Lance replies mockingly.

Suddenly, they hear an explosion. It's Lucí, who used another expansive crimson against the red demons.

"Are you sure she won't get into trouble for causing a fire in the spiritual plane?" Fatuo wonders nervously, "because doing that is illegal..."

Suddenly, a voice appears:

"Don't worry, there will be no problems."

It turns out to be Felipe, a nekosora. Nekosoras are the "carrier pigeons" of Nirma, but they are cats with wings instead of pigeons.

"Hello, Felipe," Lance greets him. "Do you have a message from my grandfather?"

"Yes, indeed. They're miuarious."

"Go ahead, cat," Fatuo demands.

"Yes. First, Lucí Fernández will be excused for the fire she caused this time."

"Really?" Lance confirms. "Phew, what a relief..."

"Yes, since no one, no innocent, was hurt, and I've sent several gammas to keep it that way... Initially, I forgive her due to her situation, which brings us to the second message..."

"What is it about?"

"The boss summons you to a meeting at his daughter's house, that is, your mother's house, Lancelot. You two, her daughter, her son-in-law, and the daughter and wife of the late Natas."

"Why would the shōgun of Nirma want a meeting with us?" Fatuo questions.

"Isn't it obvious, fireball? He wants to talk to Lucí about 'the soldiers of Purgatory.'"

A while after the massacre of red demons, Lucí is found in the spiritual realm, lying with her arms spread out on a parked car, asleep, with her face looking upwards. Fatuo and Lancelot are beside her.

"Hey, kid, why don't you kiss her to wake her up?" Fatuo teases Lancelot.

"Shut up!" Lance responds, embarrassed.

"I can't, I don't have a mouth," Fatuo mocks, "and if I did, I'd stick my tongue out at you."

"Thanks for waking me up with your silly argument," Lucí says, sitting up on the car. As she said, their bickering woke her up.

"I'm sorry, Lucí..." Lancelot apologizes, red as a tomato.

"No, seriously. After the fight with the demons and this little nap, I feel much better," Lucí tells them, de-stressed, but they start looking at her strangely. "What's wrong with you guys? Did a monkey grow on my shoulder or what?"

"It's just that, Lucí, what happened wasn't something to downplay," Fatuo explains. "You fought from 11:36 to 14:54 and exorcised 2,743 red demons. And then you took a nap on the car you're on until now, and it's already 17:24."

"Holy Carrion!" Lucí exclaims, surprised. "That means I missed lunch!"

Fatuo and Lancelot sweat drop.

"Seriously?" Fatuo questions. "That's what surprises or concerns you the most?"

"Not entirely," Lucí responds calmly. "I have some questions now that I'm calmer."

"I'm glad you're feeling better. We'll answer them on the way to my house," Lance assures but suddenly turns red again. "I... I didn't mean..."

"Lanza, it's not time to visit your house!" Lucí replies.

"What this clumsy guy meant to say was that the shōgun of Nirma summoned us to a meeting at his house," Fatuo clarifies.

"The what of Nirma?" Lucí asks. "And why at your house, Lanza?"

"It's because he's my grandfather," Lance responds, embarrassed.

"Your grandfather?" Lucí asks. "You mean 'Karate Grandpa'?"

"'Karate Grandpa'?" Fatuo says, confused. "What are you talking about?"

"I told him my grandfather was a karate master in another country," Lance tells Fatuo.

"I see, another lie..." Lucí snaps, angry. "Is at least the part about his motion sickness true?"

"That I can assure you, miss, but it doesn't matter now. We need to go quickly to that meeting with the shōgun," Fatuo states authoritatively. "We'll tell you more on the way."

"Okay, but you better give me answers!"

What a way to start! Well, while they head to that meeting, we'll check out some other consequences caused by the demon escape. We might find some things that could be important in the future, no matter how small.

As I was saying, the breakout from Tartarus caused significant problems in both worlds.

In Nirma, there were thousands of deaths from direct attacks by red demons.

On Earth, there aren't as many cases of deaths from direct attacks by them because, between their escape and arrival, an alarm was issued to the inhabitants of the terrestrial spiritual side. Still, many have perished.

But that wasn't the only problem. The red demons that arrived on Earth have been causing chaos, like an elephant in a china shop. In just a few hours, they've caused all kinds of catastrophes, from insignificant things like encouraging kids to steal candy to tornadoes and earthquakes all over the planet. It's a crisis in both worlds.

In the news, they have so much material to narrate that they're not even broadcasting the shows that usually follow.

Among the news and events, they're reporting the following:

- A meteorite crashed in the Nevada desert near Las Vegas, and despite the enormous crater it left on impact, there's no trace of the meteorite, which is déjà vu because the same thing happened in the same place about twenty years ago.
- In Mexico, a shootout broke out between two rival smuggler gangs. But when the authorities arrived, they only found dead bodies scattered on the ground. There are around forty corpses from both gangs. What baffles the officers is that, according to the forensic scientist, no more than six of the deceased had bullet wounds, but what they all have in common are huge claw marks, more significant than those of a tiger or lion. The scars are so large and deep that it seems like an elephant with claws carried out a massacre. They haven't been able to find the culprit of this mystery.
- Hunters from all over the world mysteriously faint, with no detectable injuries, while the animals they were hunting disappear without a trace.
- They report a mysterious mountain in the Himalayas that changes location as if it were a "walking mountain."

We're heading to that mountain now. It's in the middle of a monstrous snowstorm that covers it completely, which is no small feat because the darned promontory is tall enough to overshadow the Statue of Liberty.

Near its summit, the only sound is the icy storm. A loud noise like a slot machine is heard inside a cave in that area, followed by a scream.

"Grape party!"

Immediately, a river of grapes—tons of them—flows out of the cave, spills into the void, and sweeps away several demons and humans.

"I bet this will be enough to leave them without tokens," says a shrill voice, the one responsible for invoking the grape river. The voice belongs to a figure dressed like a Wild West cowboy, with a hat pulled low to cover his face. "Do you really think this will attract your friend, the bogeyman?"

Suddenly, another voice echoes throughout the cave in response:

"One, he's not my friend; he's my enemy. Two, he's not a bogeyman; he's a dragon. And three, the boss knows what he's doing."

Chapter III
A Candy Not So Sweet

It's a new day in Montevideo, a sweltering one for a summer just beginning. Fatuo is with Lance, who's wearing his armor and carrying his spear. They are heading from the spiritual plane to Lucí's house, a two-story building situated in front of the waterfront.

A few steps away from arriving, the fire demon stops and, a little discouraged, addresses his companion.

"Do you think she's ready for her job? Not even twenty-four hours have passed."

Lance responds with great confidence, "Don't worry. She's strong."

And, just as he says this, he makes a giant leap up to the balcony of Lucí's room on the second floor.

"What do you think you're doing, kid?" says Fatuo, annoyed from his initial position. "You can't just jump onto someone else's balcony, especially not a teenage girl's!"

"What are you saying? I can't hear you..." Lance responds with a slightly mocking face.

Fatuo floats up to where he is and repeats more forcefully, "You can't just jump onto someone else's balco—!"

But before he can finish the sentence, he realizes what's going on.

"You bastard, you tricked me like a baby!"

Lance bursts into laughter. Then they hear the balcony door open, and a voice says:

"Hee hee, well done, Lanza. You've learned a bit of my sense of humor. Hee hee hee."

Seeing Lucí step onto the balcony, the young man reverts to his shy personality.

"G... go... good morning, Lucí. Are you okay?"

Fatuo interrupts nervously, "Miss Lucí, I'm very sorry for being on your balcony unannounced, but this kid tricked me."

"Yes, I figured that out," Lucí says, laughing. "Apparently, he didn't tell you I asked him to meet here."

"What?" adds Fatuo, surprised and confused. "And why is that?"

Lucí looks away. "I told you in the meeting yesterday. I need some time without her."

Fatuo, a little disheartened, tries to explain, "Miss Lucí, you must understand that..."

"I know, but I feel deceived," Lucí snaps, clearly offended.

"But..." Fatuo tries to speak, but words fail him.

"I'm tired of this conversation," Lucí says, changing her mood abruptly. "Let's go after some demons..."

"Agreed... Yes, we need to work," supports Lance, who had been silent until now.

"First, you need to learn the basics," Fatuo insists.

"Basics, Fatuo? I've already killed 10,000 demons!" Lucí says proudly.

"You mean: 'Exorcised 2,743 red demons,'" Fatuo corrects her, like a mocking teacher.

"What's the difference?" Lucí asks, arms crossed.

"That's exactly what we need to talk about..." Fatuo replies, narrowing his eyes.

"Well then, spill the beans and tell me the 'basics,'" Lucí says, already annoyed.

"What beans? If I eat beans, I'd turn into steam..." Fatuo misinterprets like an idiot.

"Idiot! It's a figure of speech!" Lucí and Lance shout at the fireball in unison.

"Okay, okay, don't get mad..." Fatuo jokes but then clears his throat. "I'll start explaining, miss. Exorcising red demons is the main duty of shinigami templars (that's our profession). Red demons are the reincarnation of living beings who died with evil, hatred, resentment, or similar feelings in their hearts, or for committing atrocities in life. They can also be demons born as such but crossed over due to the same kind of feelings and actions. Red demons never fully die unless their heart heals. What you call killing isn't that; they were just sent to Tartarus for purification, which will allow them to die completely and peacefully in their hearts later."

"So, those bastards are forgiven despite everything they did?" Lucí begins to get angry at what she's hearing.

"That wouldn't be the exact word. Red demons, upon entering Tartarus, suffer attacks of thoughts from their conscience that are like torture."

"Reflecting on their actions, you call that torture?" Lucí snaps at Fatuo.

"I've seen it, and believe me, for some, it is. And once they repent, to purify themselves, they must transfer their power to the energy of Nirma, with the desire that their energy be used to make amends for their mistakes," Fatuo counters.

"After all they do, they can still die in peace?" Lucí complains.

"It's our duty, miss Lucí," he acknowledges, not very happily. "I understand that for you, comprehending this after yesterday is diffi—"

He doesn't finish his sentence because Lucí jumps from the second-floor balcony to the sidewalk, landing as if it were nothing.

"Are you done? Let's go after some of those bastards..."

"She's just like her father," Fatuo says with resignation and sadness, shaking his head.

"Well, let's follow her," Lance adds before landing next to Lucí.

"And this one's a bootlicker..." the demon mutters to himself as he floats down to join them.

"Where to now?" Lucí asks.

"We don't know. We have to take a walk around the city, on the spiritual side."

"And how do you switch to that plane?" Lucí asks again.

"You're already there; otherwise, you would have broken your heels on landing," Fatuo points out.

"I thought I'd have powers on the other side too..." she says, surprised.

"Using powers in the physical plane would be illegal. Anyway, it's impossible. The powers of demons and humans with vision, known as soulmes, don't work in the physical space due to the 'power of the border.'"

"What border?" Lucí asks, not understanding what she's hearing.

"That's what the limitation of Earth with Nirma is called. In other words, the spiritual side of Earth is that border," Fatuo continues explaining.

"Excuse me?"

"Sorry, I barely understand it myself," Fatuo apologizes. "In simple terms, the border is the spiritual side of Earth. Only there can demons inhabit (unless they have permission to enter the physical world in human disguise) and use their powers (with regulation)."

"But... but what about the red demons?"

Needless to say, Lucí is still confused.

"They always try to interfere with the physical plane of Earth, but luckily, never in history has one managed to cross over," explains Fatuo with a bit of relief.

"But what about yesterday's 'crash' with those giant frogs?" Lucí asks, gesturing backward.

"The big problem with red demons is that even though they can't cross over, their influences can. These influences are known to common humans as 'bad luck,' 'temptation,' 'accidents,' 'mistakes,' 'natural disasters'..." Fatuo begins to list.

"So, everything bad that happens in the world is because of those demons?" Lucí growls.

"Not everything, but about 9.47% of the time."

"Whatever..." she interrupts, irritated. "Anything else?"

"Yes, quite a bit more..." Fatuo responds.

"Then tell me later because I'm already bored." Lucí turns around and starts walking.

"Darn it..." Fatuo expresses with resignation.

"Let's go, Lanza and Big Fausto..." Lucí commands the two.

"Y... yes, Lucí," Lance replies timidly.

"Yes, Lucí... Big what?"

"I give nicknames to everyone I like..." Lucí responds casually.

"She likes me?" Fatuo tries to comprehend.

"Yes, we don't know each other much in person yet, but you saved my life. Not to mention what Karate Grandpa said yesterday: You've been my dad's best friend since childhood. So, you're like my uncle..." Lucí reasons.

"Mi... miss..." Fatuo gets emotional, and steam starts coming from his eyes (that's how he cries).

"And another thing, just call me Lucí. No more 'miss.'"

"Yes, Lu... Lucí," Fatuo corrects himself, still sniffling.

"By the way, Fatuo," Lance suddenly says, "behind you, there's a demon in the shape of a three-meter-tall boxer dog that, ironically, has boxing gloves and is about to punch you..."

"You idiot! Don't ruin the moment with jokes, kid!" Fatuo complains to Lance.

Suddenly, Lucí darts past Fatuo and collides her fist with the demon dog's fist...

"For fuel's sake!" Fatuo shouts, turning around and realizing it isn't a silly joke.

With their fists colliding, neither Lucí nor the dog demon intends to give in. They're evenly matched until Lancelot stabs the enemy in the back with his spear, causing it to start disintegrating into red ashes. Lucí realizes this too late, and as the red demon vanishes, she accidentally lands a small punch on her dear friend's forehead with her flaming fist, which extinguishes.

"Ouch, ouch, ouch!" Lance complains, covering the bump with one hand but not letting go of the spear with the other.

"Lu... I mean, Lucí, what are you doing!?" Fatuo exclaims in surprise and then turns to Lance. "And you, stop crying like a baby!"

"He gave the finishing blow from behind while I was facing it like a grown-up..." Lucí complains, arms crossed.

"I understand, Lucí, but you went too far. By the way, your grammar was bad," Fatuo corrects her.

"It wasn't bad grammar. It's a way of saying that if men call themselves men as a compliment to their strength and bravery, I'm also a man, end of story," Lucí expresses her opinion.

"That's fine, but not the fact that you hit the crybaby on the forehead," Fatuo reprimands her.

"I'm sorry, Lucí. I'll treat you to lunch with the money from this commission," Lance says through tears.

"Really? Thanks!" Lucí is happy, but then she realizes she doesn't understand something. "Wait, commission for what?"

"Oh, right, we forgot that part," Fatuo remembers. "When exorcising a red demon, shinigami templars receive a commission as payment from the order."

"How does that work? Explain, explain..." Lucí gets excited.

"It's true you're a bit ambitious. You see, red demons have five levels, according to their power or danger. The one you just defeated was a two-star, worth 1,500 candies," Fatuo explains.

"1,500 candies? They're going to rot their teeth," Lucí says, confused.

"No, Lucí, 'candy' is the name of the currency in Nirma," Fatuo clarifies.

"And why that name?"

"It's called candy as a reference, that for each candy (currency), you can buy a candy (sweet) in Nirma."

"What a reminder..." Lucí says, not very convinced. "Wait, what do you mean by two stars? It was hard to defeat it..."

"A two-star demon, for a novice, is no small feat, Lucí," Fatuo encourages her.

"But yesterday I defeated about five thousand," Lucí protests, unsatisfied with Fatuo's praise.

"I repeat, '2,743 red demons,' but each one was one star," Fatuo insists.

"All of them only one star?" Lucí is surprised.

"Lucí, look, no matter how weak a one-star red demon is, it's always dangerous, regardless of how strong the shinigami templar is," Fatuo continues.

"But yesterday, it was straightforward and even fun," Lucí says as if discussing a game.

"Listen, Lucí," Fatuo begins seriously. "Of all the rules you must learn from our order, you need to understand this: 'Every soul is a being, and every being can change destiny,' which is why our work is never a game."

"I know it's not a game; what a bore!" Lucí says, puffing her cheeks. "Changing the subject, how much is each star worth for red demons?"

"Well, you see, each rank of red demon is like an enemy in a video game. A one-star would be a low-level enemy, and a five-star would be like the final boss. Fortunately, there are no more than twenty of those today," Fatuo explains, a bit relieved. "Answering your question: a low-level one-star is worth 100 candies. The tougher two-star ones are worth 1,500 candies each. The mini-bosses, with three stars, are worth 20,000 candies. The bosses with four stars have rewards of 1,000,000, and finally, there are the dreaded final bosses with five stars. Their heads are worth 108,000,000 candies."

"Holy Carrion, if I keep this up, I'll become a candy distributor!" Lucí says, with money symbols practically glowing in her eyes.

"I'm telling you, it's a metaphor!" Fatuo protests.

"I don't care. If what you explained is true, I made a fortune yesterday," she starts calculating. "If each candy here is 2.5 pesos, and each one-star red demon exorcised is 100 candies, that's 250 pesos each. And since I exorcised 2,743 yesterday... I made 685,750 pesos, which is 15,947 dollars and 67 cents!"

Fatuo can't believe what he's hearing. "Seriously!? What are you, a cash register? I've never seen anyone calculate that fast!"

"When it comes to financial math, Lucí is the fastest..." Lance says, sweating a bit.

"Come on, guys, let's exorcise more red demons. I'm treating you to lunch today!" she says excitedly, starting to run.

"Should we tell her that the candies from yesterday were deducted for the fire she caused?" Fatuo murmurs to Lance worriedly.

"Later, she's happy now," Lance responds, whispering so Lucí doesn't hear. "Let her distract herself from yesterday..."

"I think you're right!" Fatuo says to Lance, understanding what he means. "Let's go patrolling!"

EDIQUID

www.ingramcontent.com/pod-product-compliance
Lightning Source LLC
LaVergne TN
LVHW091243150826
845673LV00003B/1268

* 9 7 8 9 5 6 6 4 0 4 1 2 5 *